Coloring
Book about
ADVENT

Text by Michael Goode

Illustrations by Margaret Skelly

CATHOLIC BOOK PUBLISHING CO.
NEW YORK

SEASONS OF THE YEAR

SPRING

WINTER

SUMMER

FALL

(T-690)

NIHIL OBSTAT: James T. O'Connor, S.T.D., *Censor Librorum*
IMPRIMATUR: Patrick J. Sheridan
Vicar General, Archdiocese of New York

The Nihil Obstat and Imprimatur are official declarations that a book or pamphlet is free of doctrinal or moral error.
No implication is contained therein that those who have granted the Nihil Obstat and Imprimatur agree with the contents
opinions or statements expressed.

SEASONS OF THE CHURCH YEAR

CHRISTMAS

EASTER

ORDINARY TIME

ADVENT

LENT

The Church Year has four main seasons: Advent, Chris
Lent and Easter. It also has the season of Ordinary Tim

4

ADVENT — Beginning of the Church Year

The Church seasons help us to know God and serve Him.
dvent helps us to prepare for Christ's coming at Christmas.

Jesus, God's Son, came to earth long ago. In Advent, we w̶
and prepare for Christ's coming into our hearts at Christr̶

ADVENT WREATH

An Advent wreath helps us to keep our minds on Jesus' coming. It is made of evergreen branches and has four candles.

During the four weeks before Christmas, we hang an Advent ∞ wreath in our windows or see it in our church.

ADVENT WREATH — First Candle

On the First Sunday of Advent, we light the first candle of the vreath. We begin to get excited for Christmas.

On the Second Sunday of Advent, we light the second ca[...] of the wreath. We grow more excited about Christ's comi[...]

10

VENT WREATH — Third Candle

On the Third Sunday of Advent, we light the third candle of the wreath. Now we know that Christ is very near.

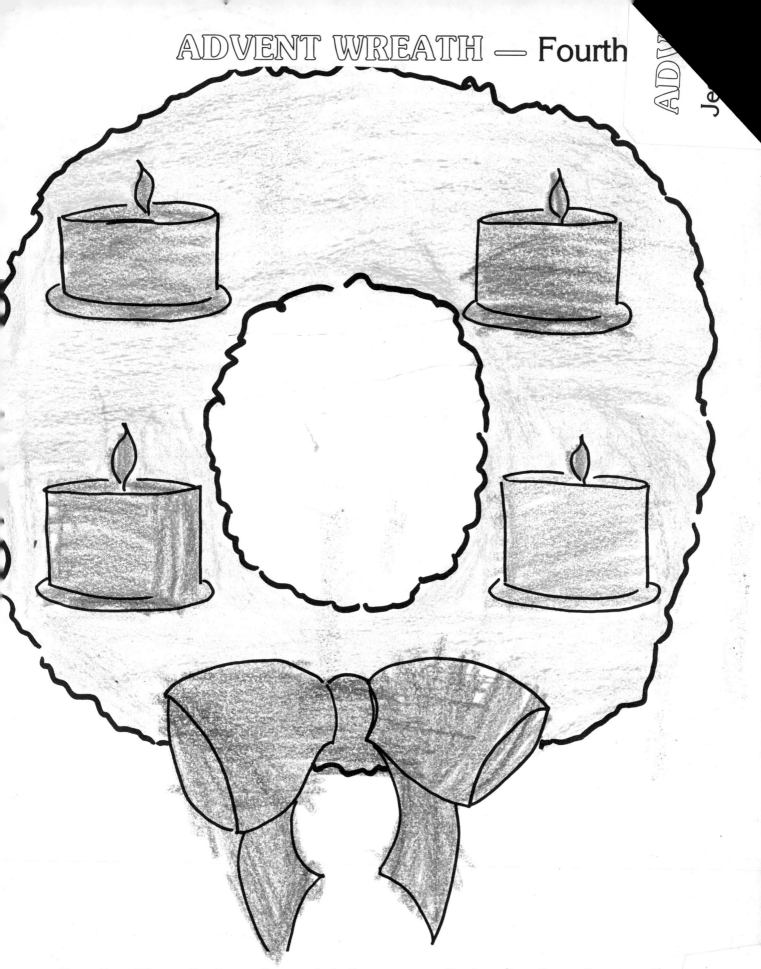

On the Fourth Sunday of Advent, we light the fourth candle the wreath. This tells us Christ is almost here.

VENT PEOPLE

sus — the Expectation of the Nations

We wait for Jesus just as the ancient peoples awaited a Divine King. The Roman poet Virgil wrote about Him.

We wait for Jesus just as the Jewish people awaited a Divi
Messiah. The great King David sang songs about Him.

14

ADVENT PEOPLE

Isaiah the Prophet

Isaiah was a great Prophet who lived many years before Christ. He had a vision of God sitting on His throne. He also spoke about God and His Messiah.

Through Isaiah, God announced that the Messiah would b
born of a Virgin. She was the Virgin Mary, Mother of Jesus.

ADVENT PEOPLE

Micah the Prophet

Micah was another Prophet of God who lived many years before Christ. He spoke about God and His Messiah.

Through Micah, God announced that the Messiah was to be born in the little town of Bethlehem.

VENT PEOPLE

The Blessed Virgin Mary

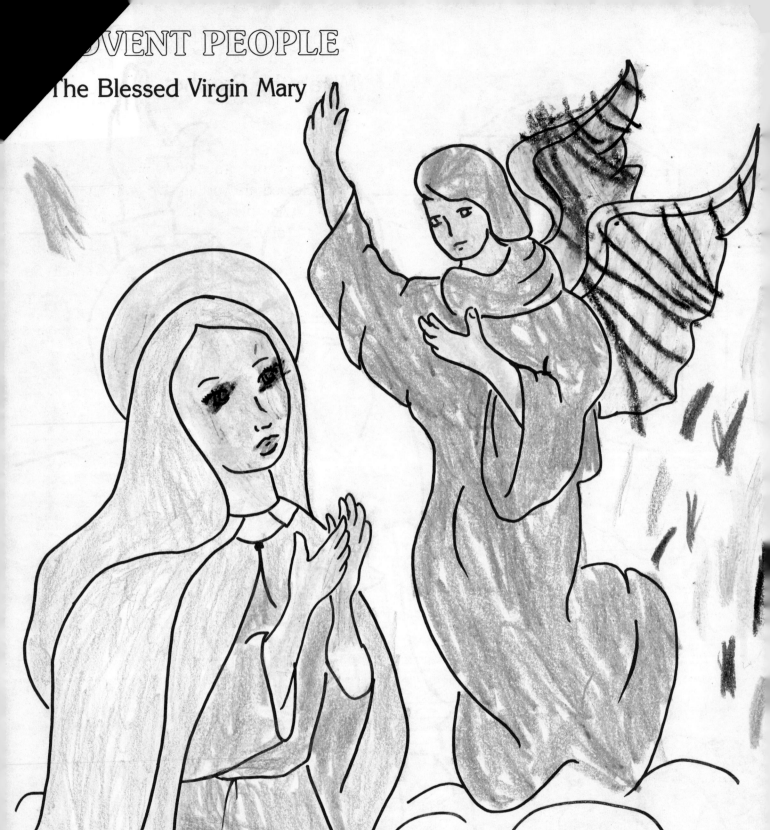

The Angel Gabriel was sent by God to a little town to a Virgin named Mary. He told her she was to be the Mother of the Messiah, who was Jesus, the Son of God.

ADVENT PEOPLE
The Blessed Virgin Mary

"Hail Mary, full of grace, the Lord is with you.
Blessed are you among women
And blessed is the Fruit
of your womb, JESUS.

Holy Mary Mother
of God,
Pray for us sinners, now,
And at the hour
of our death."
"Amen."

During Advent, we pray often to Mary. We use her favorite prayer — the HAIL MARY.

The Blessed Virgin Mary

Mary went to visit her cousin Elizabeth who was also to give birth. We celebrate this event in the Feast of the Visitation.

Mary praised God for all the good things He has done. During Advent, we praise God for all He has done for us. He has created us. He has given us our family. He has sent us Jesus.

ADVENT PEOPLE

John the Baptist

Elizabeth gave birth to a son who was called John the Baptist.

He was to be the herald of Jesus the Messiah.

When John the Baptist grew up, he prepared the way for Jesus the Messiah. During Advent, we prepare for Christ's coming into our hearts at Christmas.

ADVENT VIRTUES
Praying

During Advent, we try to say our prayers with more meaning.
We try to think of Jesus more often, even when we are playing.

During Advent, we should pray: "Lord Jesus, I love You. Prepare my soul to receive You at Christmas."

The Holy Bible is the Word of God. It was written by holy people over a long period of time. It tells us many wonderful things about God and His Son Jesus.

Reading God's Word

During Advent, we try to read Bible stories more often. We learn about Jesus and prepare to receive Him at Christmas.

ADVENT VIRTUES

Hope

Hope helps us to believe that God will always take care of our souls. During Advent, we wait with hope, for Jesus is coming.

ADVENT VIRTUES
Hope

We recall Christ's coming in History. He went about doing good and preaching the Good News of salvation for all who are faithful to Him. He loves all children.

ADVENT VIRTUES

Hope

We wait for Christ's coming **in Mystery**. This coming takes place especially at Christmas when He comes into our hearts.

Hope

We look forward to Christ's coming <u>in Glory</u>. This coming will take place at the end of the world.

Rejoice and
Be Glad!
Christmas
Is Here!